SUPERMARKET

steeple

church

sidewalk

grocer

butcher

customer

fire hydrant

windshield

headlight

Sergeant Murphy

pickle car

motorcycle

tire

milk truck

street sign

MAIN STREET

OKAY SQUARE

pole

POST OFFICE

FIRE COMPANY

sign

TAXI

TAXI STAND

mail van

fire engine

fire fighter

P9-DZN-940

Richard Scarry's
Best FIRST

RANDOM HOUSE 🏠 NEW YORK

Copyright © 1979 by Richard Scarry. All rights reserved under International and Pan-American Copyright Conventions. Published in the United States by Random House, Inc., New York, and simultaneously in Canada by Random House of Canada Limited, Toronto. *Library of Congress Cataloging in Publication Data.* Scarry, Richard. Richard Scarry's best first book ever. SUMMARY: Introduces the alphabet, counting, shapes and sizes, colors, parts of the body, months of the year, manners, nursery rhymes, and more. [1. Vocabulary. 2. Animals—Fiction] I. Title. PZ7.S327Rh 428'.1 79-3900 ISBN 0-394-84250-2 ISBN 0-394-94250-7 (lib. bdg.) Manufactured in the United States of America 2 3 4 5 6 7 8 9 0

BOOK EVER!

Huckle Cat and Lowly Worm...

HELP WITH THE HOUSEWORK	VISIT THE DOCTOR
GO TO SCHOOL	LOOK AT A FARM
PLAY IN THE PLAYGROUND	DRIVE TO THE HARBOR
SHOP AT THE SUPERMARKET	STOP AT THE RAILROAD STATION

...and More!

They Learn About...

COLORS	THE ALPHABET
MANNERS	COUNTING
PARTS OF THE BODY	SHAPES
MONTHS OF THE YEAR	SIZES

...and More Than 700 Words!

This is the house of the Cat family—
Daddy, Mommy, Huckle, and Sally.
Their friend Lowly Worm often comes
to spend the night.

roof

side of the house

bush

Huckle Cat's bedroom

Huckle

blanket

bed

Sally Cat

bathroom

upstairs hall

Lowly Worm

clock

sink

back door

cabinets

stove

kitchen floor

table

stairs

chimney

attic window

The sun is coming up.
It is almost daylight.
Wake up, Cat family!

Daddy Cat

lamp

Mommy Cat

closet

weather vane

rising sun

picture

candle

vase

fireplace

logs

television

garage

hat

car

rug

books

bookcase

sofa

front door

living room

front lawn

Mr. Frumble

table

mirror

medicine chest

The Cat family wakes up.
They take turns using
the bathroom.

glass

Daddy Cat washes
his face.

shower

soap

bathrobe

towel

faucet

wash basin

Mommy Cat takes
a shower.

shower curtain

Huckle brushes
his teeth.

bathtub

pajamas

comb

bath mat

toothpaste

perfume

talcum powder

shampoo

Sally combs her hair.

nightgown

slippers

And Lowly Worm weighs himself.
How much do you weigh, Lowly?

scale

toilet

Now they all get dressed.

bonnet

Daddy puts on his best blue suit and his favorite red necktie.

hat

cap

jacket

pants

shoes

shirt

Huckle wears a yellow shirt. He pulls on his red overalls.

underpants

socks

sneakers

My! Doesn't Sally look nice in her green jumper and black shoes?

Lowly ties his one shoelace.

Mommy Cat is having a hard time deciding what to wear.
She finally decides to wear a skirt and a blouse.

scarf

handkerchief

slip

slacks

skirt   blouse   sweater

dress

purse

stockings

pocketbook

shoes   boots   sandals

salad bowl

refrigerator

wall cabinet

jar

can

box

ice cubes

eggs

milk

meat

door

cheese

bottles

lettuce

dust mop

freezer

MARCH

calendar

clock

shopping list

pencil

coffeepot

teapot

fork

plate

sugar bowl

chair

napkin

knife

spoon

pepper

salt

tablecloth

pitcher

egg beater

grater

bottle opener

cereal bowl

wire whisk

Breakfast in the Kitchen

Mommy is frying bacon and eggs.
Sally is making toast.
Huckle is pouring milk into his cereal bowl.
Oh dear! Lowly fell in! Hurry,
Huckle! Wash him off in the sink.

Mr. Frumble

curtains

stove hood

bread

rolls

scale

iron

jug

ironing board

saucepan

laundry basket

cutting board

table

mug

eggcup

frying pan

tea kettle

burned toast

glass

cup

burner

saucer

apron

sponge

dish soap

toaster

eggshells

butter

food grinder

sink

faucet

brush

strainer

measuring spoons

rolling pin

ladle

spatula

colander

carving knife

paring knife

Housework

After breakfast everyone helps with the housework. Lowly helps clear the table. Be careful, Lowly. Daddy washes the dishes.

keys

juicer

garbage pail

pots and pans

Sally sweeps the floor.

Huckle holds the dustpan.

pail of water

lamp

broom

dustpan

scrub brush

liquid soap

Mommy washes the laundry.
The washing machine is leaking, Mommy.
Daddy slips on the wet floor.

mop

watch

shelf

washing machine

laundry basket

Sally will mop up the water.

After Lowly made all the beds,
his own bed looked so nice that he
decided to take a nap.
Daddy is vacuuming the living-room
carpet. My! That vacuum cleaner
certainly is hungry!
Sally dusts all over.

staircase

umbrella stand

chest

chair

feather
duster

television

record player

telephone

books

camera

magazines

bookcase

Huckle empties
the wastebasket.

radio

Mommy is sewing a shirt for Lowly.

sewing
machine

spool of thread

pins

buttons

pin cushion

thimble

safety pin

scissors

table

tape measure

rose

vase

thumbtacks

pushpin

bell

map

umbrella

lost
sneaker

notice

boot

bulletin board

pad of paper

ruler

pencil
sharpener

ball-point pen

singer

Miss Honey

piano

table

At School

Huckle, Sally, and Lowly
go to school. They do many
things at school.

This morning, Miss Honey,
the teacher, is playing
a tune on the piano and
singing a song.

coloring
book

embroidery

crayons

paste

scrapbook

footprint

sheet of paper

stool

water dish

paint box

scraps of paper

arithmetic lesson

spelling lesson

chalk

chalkboard

eraser

Mr. Frumble

writing on the chalkboard

reading
a picture book

stringing beads

sink

Janitor Joe keeps
the schoolhouse neat
and clean.
Ooops! He slipped
on a bead.

mop

pail of water

wastebasket

pencil

eraser

marker pen

sticky tape

paint jars

picture

a picture
painter

Sizes

Miss Honey is teaching the children about sizes and shapes. Just look at all the sizes and shapes in the schoolroom.

Miss Honey is big.

Bug is little.

Mr. Frumble's hat is not too big and not too small. It is medium.

Mr. Frumble is fat.

Lowly is thin.

Mouse has a short nose.

Elephant has a long nose.

Some books are wide.

Some books are narrow.

Elephant has thick legs.

Spoonbill has thin legs.

Some pupils are tall.

Some pupils are short.

Big Hilda is huge.

Bugdozer is tiny.

This cap is the right size.

This cap is too large.

Shapes

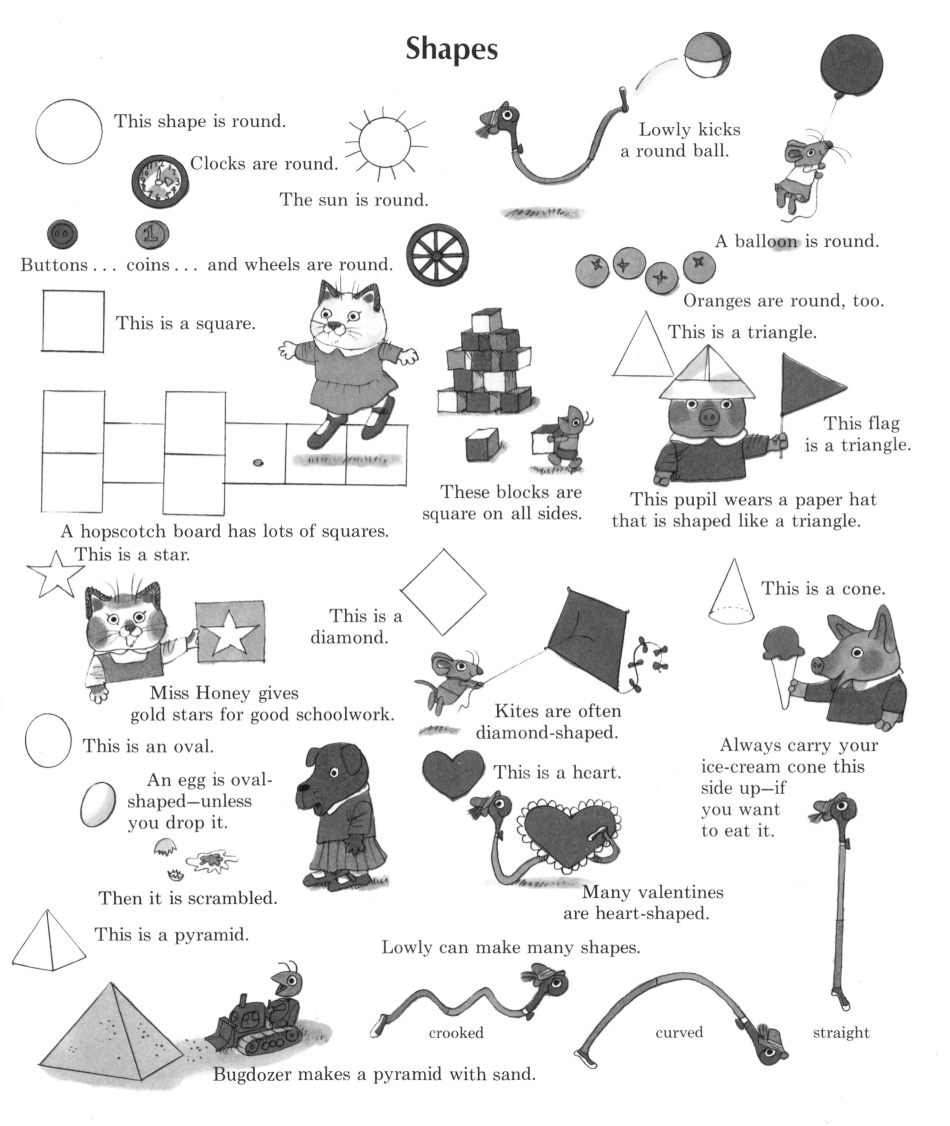

This shape is round.

Clocks are round.

The sun is round.

Lowly kicks a round ball.

A balloon is round.

Buttons . . . coins . . . and wheels are round.

Oranges are round, too.

This is a square.

This is a triangle.

These blocks are square on all sides.

This flag is a triangle.

This pupil wears a paper hat that is shaped like a triangle.

A hopscotch board has lots of squares.

This is a star.

This is a diamond.

This is a cone.

Miss Honey gives gold stars for good schoolwork.

Kites are often diamond-shaped.

This is an oval.

This is a heart.

Always carry your ice-cream cone this side up—if you want to eat it.

An egg is oval-shaped—unless you drop it.

Then it is scrambled.

Many valentines are heart-shaped.

This is a pyramid.

Lowly can make many shapes.

Bugdozer makes a pyramid with sand.

crooked

curved

straight

At the Playground

At recess Miss Honey takes the children outside to play in the schoolyard. No one stays inside the schoolhouse.
What is everyone doing?

Janitor Joe swinging way up high

Joe's mop and pail falling down

Sally is playing with a jump rope.

hanging upside down

sliding down the pole

climbing up the ladder

This looks like a game of leapfrog.

leaping over

These children are playing ring-around-the-rosy.

Two children are playing a game of tag.

up

crouching under

in back

in front

This is a seesaw.

down

These pupils are wrestling— and getting dirty!

Two teams are playing tug of war.

top of slide

losers

winners

Miss Honey takes a turn
sliding down the slide.

kick

bottom of slide

inside
the barrel

Lowly is
playing
hide-and-seek.

outside the barrel

ball

on the left   in the middle   on the right

catch

Three children are standing side by side.

throw

miss   hit

somersaulting over

playhouse

Two pupils are
in the sandbox.

Is Mr. Frumble still
chasing his hat?
Catch it, Mr. Frumble!

going in   coming out

The Alphabet

A a — airplane

B b — boat

C c — crab

D d — dog

E e — engine

F f — Frumble

G g — goose

H h — hen

I i — igloo

J j — jeep

K k — kangaroo

L l — letter

M m — motorcycle

N n
nurse

O o
owl

P p
penguin

Q q
queen

R r
rooster

S s
sparrow

T t
turtle

U u
umbrella

V v
van

W w
wolf

X x
xylophone

Y y
yak

Z z
zebra

After recess Lowly reads his ABC book.
Do you know your ABC's?

Counting

Mommy and Daddy pick
up the children after school.
They have many errands
to do before going home.
The children practice
counting along the way.

1 one window washer

2 two police officers

3 three street cleaners

4 four schoolchildren waiting for their buses

BUS 1   BUS 2   BUS 3   BUS 4

5 five bicycle riders

6 six painters

7 seven letter carriers

8 eight pencil cars

9 nine bug taxis

10 ten fire fighters putting out a fire

My! What a lot of fire fighters!

Colors

On the way to town, Huckle and Lowly see cars and trucks of many different colors. Their own car is orange.

a red fire engine

a yellow bananamobile

an orange school bus

a green watermelon truck

Red and yellow make orange.

Blue and yellow make green.

Red and blue make purple.

Red and white make pink.

a blue police car

a purple tractor and grape wagon

a brown dump truck

a pink jeep

a green hat

a black-and-white taxi

a rainbow pencil car

a gray cherry-picker truck

a white ambulance

Red, yellow, blue, and
black make brown.

Black and white make gray.

FRUITS

bananas

Grocer Dog

lemons

apples

oranges

cherries

grapefruit

grapes

pickle barrel

pears

melons

strawberries

blueberries

raspberries

pineapple

At the Supermarket

watermelon

The Cat family stops at the supermarket. Daddy buys fresh fruit and vegetables from the grocer.

Mommy buys some meat from the butcher.

hook

saw

ham

meat cleaver

meat grinder

bacon

frankfurters

hamburger

chop

string

steak

bologna

knife

apron

knife sharpener

roll of paper

sawdust

VEGETABLES

cash register

peaches

corn

lettuce

beans

peas

celery

radishes

squash

plums

tomatoes

beets

carrots

cucumbers

cabbage

onions

turnip

cauliflower

*Say there, Mr. Frumble!
Watch where you're going!*

sack of potatoes

pumpkin

peanut butter

sardines

nuts

mustard

syrup

eggs

ketchup

spaghetti

cookies

cherry pie

raisins

jam

can of tomato soup

honey

ice cream

olives

jelly

shopping cart

orangeade

cheese

salt

sugar

Good and Bad Manners

After putting their groceries into the car, the Cat family decides to go to the ice-cream parlor for a treat. There they meet Mrs. Pig and her two boys.

"How do you do, Mrs. Pig?" says Huckle. "I would do much better if Bop and Bonk would stop fighting and mind their manners," says Mrs. Pig.

Lowly sits up straight in his chair like a good worm.

Sally says politely, "Please pass the cookies."

When Huckle is served, he says, "Thank you."

Bop and Bonk fight over who is going to have which chair. *Naughty boys!*

Lowly eats slowly and quietly.

Bop gobbles his ice cream and makes awful noises.

Bonk doesn't ask someone to pass the cookies. He reaches over to get them and knocks over Bop's juice.

Bonk guzzles his juice and spills it all over his shirt. You should take smaller sips, Bonk!

Mrs. Pig is talking to Mommy Cat. Bop keeps interrupting his mother, which is not very nice manners.

Huckle has more cherries than Sally. He shares his cherries with her.

Bonk steals the cherries from Bop's ice cream. What an awful thing to do!

Don't rock back and forth in your chair, Bonk! It is not good manners.

He rocks too far and grabs the tablecloth.

Bonk clears the table. What terrible manners!

And what a mess! You will have to teach your boys better manners, Mrs. Pig.

As he leaves, Lowly says, "It was nice to meet you, Mrs. Pig. And good luck with your manners lessons."

A Visit to the Doctor

Today Huckle has an appointment for a physical checkup with Dr. Bones.

Lowly steps on the scale.
"You have put on a lot of weight since the last time you were here, Lowly," says Nurse Nora.

After Huckle takes off his clothes, Dr. Bones listens to Huckle's heart through his stethoscope.
"Your heart is thumping very nicely, Huckle," says Dr. Bones.

Dr. Bones measures Huckle's height.
"My, you are growing tall," he says.
"You must be eating everything your mother serves you."

Next Dr. Bones checks Huckle's eyesight.
"I can see everything on the chart," says Huckle.
"You have very good eyes," says Dr. Bones.

medicine

scissors

tweezers

cotton balls

bandages

adhesive tape

plastic bandage

flashlight

thermometer

tongue depressor

"I must give you a shot to keep you well and healthy," says Dr. Bones. "It may hurt a little bit, but only for a second."
It doesn't hurt too much.

Then Dr. Bones looks at Huckle's throat.
He also looks down Lowly's throat.
"Say AH-H-H, Lowly."
Lowly says, "AH-H-H."
"You have a very nice long throat, Lowly."

Dr. Bones taps on Huckle's back.
He looks in Huckle's ears. He squeezes Huckle's tummy a little bit.
"That tickles," says Huckle.

"Well, Huckle," says Dr. Bones, "it has been a pleasure to examine such a fine, healthy boy as you. You may get dressed now."

As Huckle and Lowly leave, Dr. Bones says, "Keep eating properly and I am sure that you will be much bigger on your next visit."
"Good-bye, and thank you, Dr. Bones."

The Parts of the Body

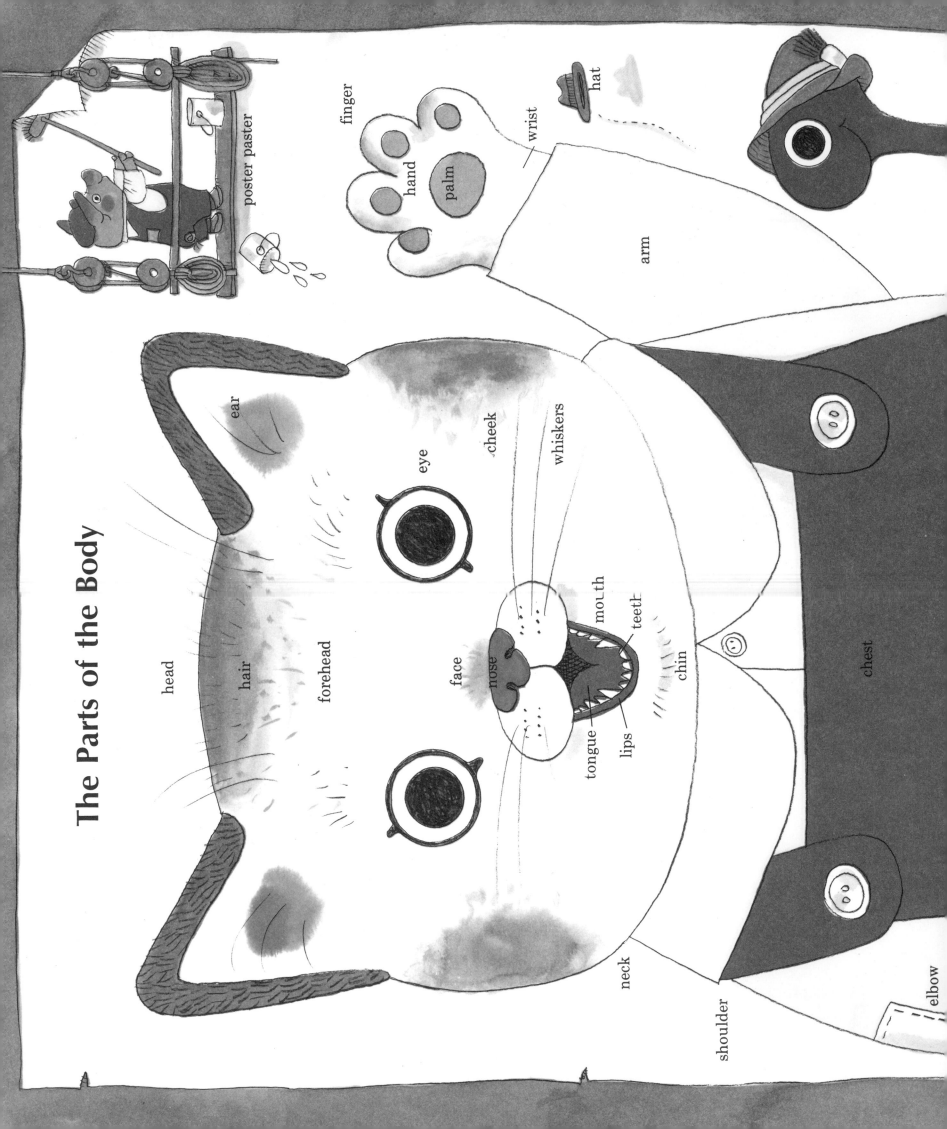

poster paster

finger

wrist

hat

hand

palm

arm

ear

eye

cheek

whiskers

head

hair

forehead

face

nose

mouth

teeth

chin

tongue

lips

chest

neck

shoulder

elbow

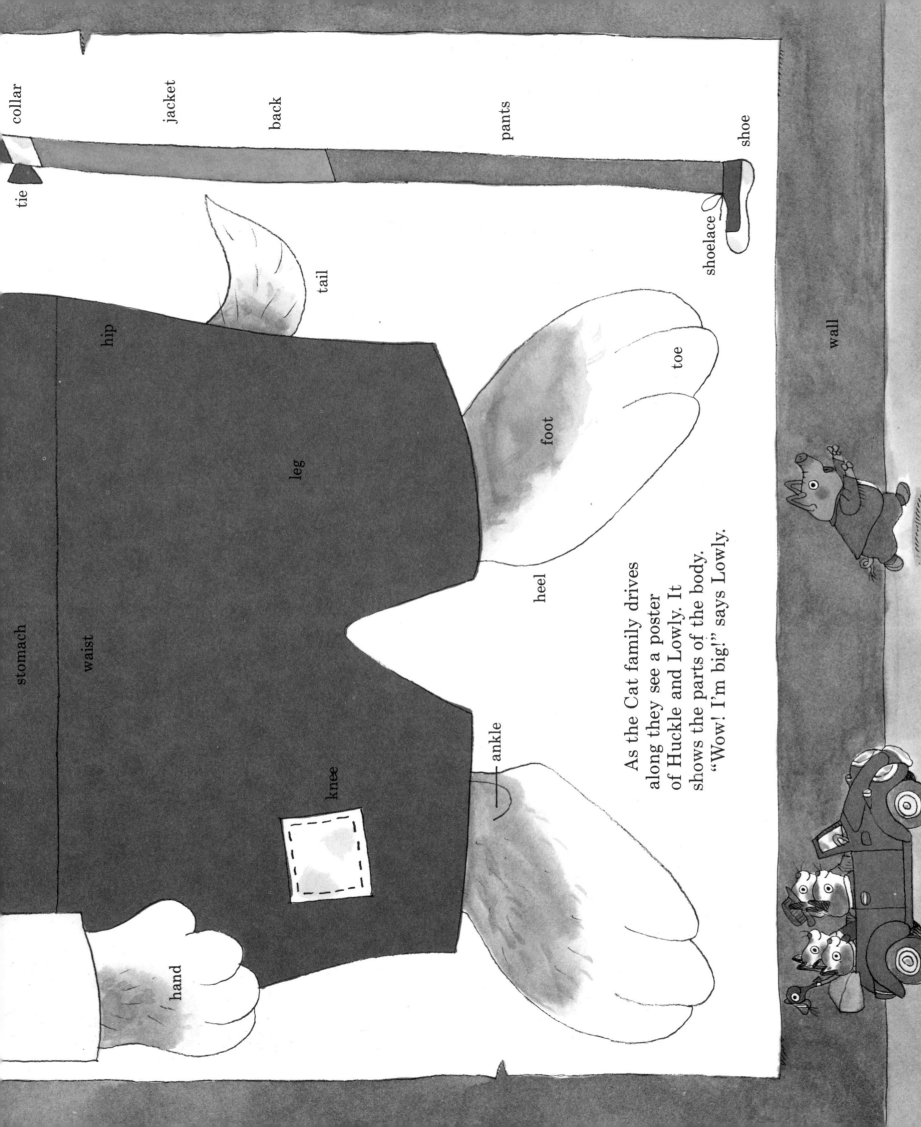

collar

jacket

back

pants

shoe

tie

shoelace

tail

hip

toe

wall

leg

foot

heel

stomach

waist

ankle

knee

hand

As the Cat family drives along they see a poster of Huckle and Lowly. It shows the parts of the body. "Wow! I'm big!" says Lowly.

windmill

forest

apple tree

brook

grain harvester

chimney

"Let's visit Farmer Pig and his family and see what they are doing," says Daddy.

My! What a busy farm. They are growing all kinds of things to eat.

farmhouse

water pump

apple pie

ax

woodpile

grass cutter

"But where are all your children, Mrs. Pig? And what are they doing?" asks Daddy.

"They are all in the next field," says Mrs. Pig. "Come, I will show you what they are doing."

a pick-up truck that backed up too far

stream

Action Words

Farmer and Mrs. Pig certainly have a lot of children. And they are all doing something.

eating

drinking

standing

sitting

lying down

holding and smelling

riding

pushing

pulling

talking

listening

kneeling

laughing

smiling

frowning

crying

walking

running

jumping

shouting

whispering

giggling

tripping

hiding

reading

writing

drawing

watching

falling

giving

taking

digging

building

pointing

looking

sewing

blowing

singing and dancing

kicking

kissing

hugging

wrestling

Lowly is wriggling.

And what is Mr. Frumble doing?
Why, Mr. Frumble is still
chasing his hat!
I wonder if he will ever catch it.

At the Harbor

barge

smokestack

towline

tugboat

sailboat

submarine

rowboat

lighthouse

rocks

pier

buoy

"We mustn't forget to stop at
the fish market," says Mommy.
"I haven't forgotten," says Daddy.
"Here we are at the harbor now."

speeding
motorboat

water taxi

fishing boat

Mr. Frumble

Mommy buys fresh fish for supper.
"That is the last of our shopping,"
she says. "Now we can go straight home."

a fisherman mending his net

net

crane

anchor

lifeboat

cargo ship

smoke

fire

fire fighters

life raft

fireboat

captain

police boat

flag

My! What a busy harbor.

car ferry

dock

powerboat

The Railroad Station

On the way home, the Cat family has to pass the railroad station. As they approach the crossing, the guards crank down the crossing gates.

STOP! Two trains are coming into the station!

control tower

crossing gate

BAGGAG

road

station platform

railroad tracks

fried eggs

waiter

COACH

RESTAURANT CAR

APPLE CIDER

roadside stand

CAT

warning sign

railroad station

BUSYTOWN

RESTAURANT

TICKETS

repair worker

signal tower

boxcar

mail sacks

steam
locomotive

MAIL

diesel locomotive

bumper

fork-lift truck

paint roller

wrench

pliers

paint

brush

electric drill

plane

shelf

cord

saw

screwdriver

tape measure

brace and bit

plug

tricycle

hammer

ax

screws

nut

bolt

nail

shovel

board

string

Daddy fixes things in his workshop.

Lowly is making a boat.

nails

The Cat family arrives home at last.
But there are still many chores to do around the house.
Daddy has asked some workers to come over and help.

watering can

clover

hoe

flowerpot

faucet

crocus

daffodil

trowel

hose

tulip

pansies

hyacinth

strawberry

bluebells

violets

roses

bug

lilies of the valley

daisies

Mommy waters the flowers in her garden.
Watch what you're doing, Mommy.

sunflower

leaf

leaves

branch

trunk

tree

Sally picks
a basket
of flowers.

sack

flower basket

Freddy Fox is on
the stepladder picking
apples from the
apple tree.
I hope he doesn't
hurt himself.

stepladder

rock

*Oh dear! Mr. Frumble
is still trying to catch his hat!*

dandelion weed

The boy from next-door is
mowing the lawn for Daddy.

Huckle rakes
the cut grass.

watch

grass

dirt

lawn mower

wheelbarrow

wagon

Mother Goose Rhymes

When supper is finished,
it is nighttime.
Then Daddy reads some
Mother Goose rhymes to
Sally, Huckle, and Lowly.

Tom, Tom, the piper's son,
Stole a pig and away did run.
The pig was eat, and Tom was beat,
And Tom went crying down the street.

Doctor Foster went to Gloucester
In a shower of rain.
He stepped in a puddle,
Right up to his middle,
And never went there again.

Jack, be nimble.
Jack, be quick.
Jack, jump over
The candlestick.

Jack Sprat could eat no fat,
His wife could eat no lean,
And so between them both, you see,
They licked the platter clean.

Little Miss Muffet
Sat on a tuffet,
Eating her curds and whey;
Along came a spider,
Who sat down beside her,
And frightened Miss Muffet away.

Jack and Jill went up the hill
    To fetch a pail of water;
Jack fell down and broke his crown,
    And Jill came tumbling after.

Georgie Porgie, pudding and pie,
Kissed the girls and made them cry;
When the boys came out to play,
Georgie Porgie ran away.

Mr. Frumble

Good night,
Sleep tight,
Wake up bright
In the morning light.

Then, after a very busy day,
everyone gets ready for bed.
    Look! Mommy has fallen
asleep already!
    Good night, Mommy.

picture book

doll

newspaper

There are twelve months in a year.

January
January is the month for coasting down snowy hills.

February
In February we give valentines to the ones we love.

March
When strong March winds blow, you should hold on to your hat.

April
Don't get wet in the April showers.

May
In May, flowers are blooming everywhere. Huckle gives a bouquet of flowers to his mother.

June
It is nice to take a drive in the country in June.